I0530885

The House on River Road

W.D. Frolick

Author: W.D. Frolick

Publisher: WDF Publishing

Website: www.wdfpublishing.com

Paperback ISBN 978-1-7751958-4-9

E-Book ISBN 978-1-7751958-5-6

First Edition Copyright © 2019 by W.D. Frolick. All rights reserved.

Revised Edition March 2023

No part of this book may be reproduced in any form or by any electronic or mechanical means, including information storage and retrieval systems, without permission in writing from the publisher, except by a reviewer who may quote brief passages in a review. The characters, locations, and events in this book are fictitious, and any similarity to persons living or dead is purely coincidental and is not intended by the author.

Cover and formatting by bookdesign.ca

Contents

Summer of 1951

My name is David Fairburn. I was born in the village of Little Muddy Water almost eleven years ago. My father owns a general store on Main Street, and we live in an apartment above the store.

Located on the banks of Little Muddy River and the shores of Lake Muddy Water, our town has a population of 945.

Unfortunately, there's not much for kids to do in Little Muddy Water, especially during summer vacation. My friends and I get bored, and sometimes our fun becomes mischief. Mischief gets us into trouble with our parents and occasionally with our policeman, Mr. Roy Tindell.

Even though it was a warm July evening, a cold chill snaked down my spine. I was staring at the old, dilapidated house on River Road—the place rumored to be haunted.

I turned to my best friend, Walter Fisher, and asked, "What do you think, Wally, is the house haunted?"

He looked at me with fear in his brown eyes and replied, "It could be. Everyone says that, but I don't think I wanna find out."

"What are you, a scared little mouse?"

Wally laughed nervously and said, "Just throw me a piece of cheese, and you'll soon find out."

Suddenly, the empty antique rocking chair on the veranda began to move back and forth.

"Did you see that?" I whispered.

"Yeah, I did. There isn't any breeze. Why is the chair rockin'?" Wally whispered back.

"I don't know," I said, "but I'd like to find out."

"Let's get the heck outta here," Wally said.

"Not so fast," I said. "There must be a logical explanation."

"Yeah, there is. The house is haunted," Wally said, his eyes growing wider.

"I don't believe you. Let me prove it. Why don't we plan to spend a night inside? We can each bring a flashlight, a sleeping bag, and snacks. Maybe Chookie will join us, and we'll be the Three Musketeers on an adventure."

"You gotta be crazy, David," Wally said with a nervous laugh. "I've seen all the proof I need. Let's go before the mosquitoes come out and eat us alive."

Reluctantly I agreed, and we headed for home.

The following day at breakfast, I asked my dad, "Do you think the old house on River Road is haunted?"

"That's what everyone seems to think, David. Why do you ask?"

"Wally and I checked it out last night, and it sure looks spooky to me."

"You didn't go inside, did you?"

"No. We looked at it from the road."

"That's good. I don't want you or your friends anywhere near that place. It's scheduled to be demolished in a few weeks. It's old, and it could be unsafe. The floorboards are probably rotted out, and you could fall into the basement and hurt yourself."

"Why are they tearing it down, Dad?"

"Because the village owns the house and has tried to sell it for over a year without any offers. Rumors the house is haunted have kept prospective buyers away. Once the house is demolished, the council agrees they will have no trouble selling the vacant land."

"How come the village owns the house, Dad?"

"The owner, Clarence Crookshank, died without relatives and didn't leave a will. Because he owed several years of unpaid property taxes, the village of Little Muddy Water became the legal owner."

"Is it true Mr. Crookshank died in the house a few years ago, and they didn't find his body for over a week?"

"That's the story I heard. Originally, the coroner believed Clarence Crookshank had died from a heart attack. Mr. Crookshank was eighty-five years old. But later, the coroner changed his report and said the cause of death was unknown."

"That's weird. I wonder why the coroner did that?" I asked.

"I don't know, but Dr. Bazooky told me the coroner said he was sure old Clarence had died from fright. He said there was no proof, so I guess that's why he changed the report to read the cause of death was unknown."

"Do you believe that story, Dad?"

"I don't know what to believe, David, but promise me you'll stay away from that house."

"Okay," I lied. "I'll stay away. Is it true that Mrs. Crookshank drowned in the river?"

"Yes. Clarence's wife supposedly drowned a year or so before he died, but her body was never found."

"Do you know what happened?"

"According to Mr. Crookshank, he and his wife decided to go fishing one afternoon. Clarence kept his old wooden rowboat on the river bank behind his house. They were anchored in the middle of the river when Mrs. Crookshank latched on to a huge northern pike. A non-swimmer, Mrs. Crookshank, stood up to try and land the fish. She lost her balance, fell into the swift-flowing water, and disappeared in seconds. Clarence, who wasn't a good swimmer, decided to stay in the boat. He pulled up the anchor, rowed to shore, and ran to the police station. It took a few hours to assemble a search party. Several boats searched the river until dark, and for two days, the river was dragged without finding Mrs. Crookshank. To this day, she is still missing."

"I wonder how come Mrs. Crookshank was never found?" I asked.

"I don't know, David. However, a story circulated around town saying that the police suspected that Clarence Crookshank didn't tell the truth about what happened to his wife."

"What do you mean?"

"Clarence was known for his bad temper. The police suspected he might have murdered his wife and buried her body. They obtained a warrant and searched the property, but Eva Crookshank's body was never found. The police couldn't charge old Clarence because they had no evidence that a crime had been committed."

"Do you think that's what happened to poor Mrs. Crookshank?"

"I don't know, David. It's a mystery that may never be solved."

After breakfast, I went to call on my second-best friend, Marvin Morris. His mom told me that Marvin went fishing and was at the town pier. When I arrived, he was sitting on the edge of the dock wearing rubber boots, a baseball cap on his head, and a fishing rod in his hand.

"Hi, Chookie," I said. Chookie was Marvin's nickname.

"Oh, hi, Butch," Marvin said, surprised to see me. Butch was my nickname.

"Catch any fish?" I asked.

He bent down and pulled up a stringer with three nice walleye attached.

"It looks like you'll have fish for supper," I said.

"Yeah, my mom will be happy if I clean 'em."

"Hey," I said. "Do you wanna go on an adventure?"

"What kind of adventure?"

"A sleepover," I replied.

"A sleepover? Where? At your house?"

"No. At the house on River Road."

"Do you mean the Crookshank house? The haunted house?"

"Yeah. Are you game?"

"Are you crazy? That place is creepy."

"That's what Wally said. Where's your sense of adventure?"

"Sittin' here fishin' is all the adventure I need."

"Don't be chicken. It'll be fun."

"Yeah, as much fun as havin' a tooth pulled."

Chookie set his fishing rod down, jumped up, and started to cluck like an old mother hen. He began to run around in a circle, flapping his arms like a pair of wings.

I laughed so hard that tears filled my eyes and rolled down my cheeks.

"Chookie," I said, "you should become a comedian when you grow up."

"At least it would be safer than becomin' a ghost hunter. As a comedian, I might have to dodge a few ripe tomatoes or rotten eggs, but that wouldn't be half as bad as being scared to death."

Just then, there was a sharp tug on Chookie's line, and the rod flew off the dock, disappearing into the muddy water.

"How come the line didn't play out?" I asked.

"Because I had the brake on. My dad is gonna kill me. My parents gave me that rod and reel last month for my eleventh birthday," Chookie said, choking back tears.

"Your dad will never have to know. Go to the hardware store and talk to Mr. Lemon. He'll replace your rod and reel and will let you pay it off from your monthly allowance. He let me pay for a new pair of skates that way last year, and I'm sure he'll do the same for you."

"I hope you're right."

"Gettin' back to our adventure," I said, "if Wally agrees to go, will you come with us?"

"I guess. If Wally goes, I'll go, but I'm still not excited about the idea of sleepin' in a haunted house."

"I doubt it's haunted. But that's what I intend to find out."

"When do you wanna go?"

"How about Saturday night?"

"Okay, but what are we gonna tell our parents?"

"You can tell your mom and dad you're sleeping at my place in a tent in our backyard," I said.

"Okay. I'll tell my parents I'm sleepin' over at your house, and Wally can say the same to his mom and dad."

"Swear you won't tell anyone our plans. Okay?"

"Okay. I swear," Chookie said.

"Cross your heart," I said.

Chookie crossed his heart.

"Good. I'm heading over to Wally's. Let's meet at my house at ten on Friday morning. We can go to the hideout and make plans for Saturday night."

"Okay. See you later."

"Oh, no," I cringed, "look who's coming."

Chookie turned his head and saw Terry Toy, our nemesis and school bully, walking toward us with his hands stuffed in his pockets and a devilish smirk on his broad face.

"What's up, Stooges?" Terry growled.

Terry Toy was bigger and taller than most kids his age and had a mean streak a mile long. A week before school ended, he followed Marvin, Wally, and me on our way home. For some unknown reason, he enjoyed taunting us. Because Marvin and Wally were a little chubby, he called them "Chunky" and "Walrus." Since I'm skinny, he called me "Bones."

The day Terry followed us from school, he kept repeating, "Chunky, Walrus, and Bones—the Three Stooges." The constant badgering finally got to Chookie. He turned abruptly and tackled Terry, lifting him off his feet. Terry punched Chookie hard on his head, knocking him out colder than a January morning. Terry pushed Chookie away and jumped to his feet. I ran at Terry, took a wild swing, and missed. Terry's fist connected with my forehead, and I saw a cluster of stars as I hit the ground. All this time, Wally watched as Chookie and I got punched. Not wanting to be Terry's next victim, he turned and ran for the safety of his home. Terry took off after Wally. Wally wasn't the fastest runner, but neither was Terry. Wally's head start got him home a few seconds before Terry could lay a beating on him.

I asked, "What do you want, T.T.?" T.T. was what we called Terry; he thought it stood for Terry Toy. But to us, it stood for "Terrible Terry."

"I just wanted to see how you Stooges are enjoyin' summer vacation. Where's your friend Wally Walrus, the third Stooge?"

"None of your business, Toy," Chookie said defiantly.

"Watch your mouth, Chunky, or you'll get a knuckle sandwich," Terry shouted.

"Got nothing better to do, Terry?" I asked.

"Yeah, I do, Baldy. I'm goin' to see Sion Johansen, the pretty girl from our class you've got a crush on. I'm takin' her to a movie on Friday night, and I'll be kissin' her in the back row. I probably won't even get to see the movie. Eat your heart out, sucker. See you later, Stooges."

Terry hadn't called me Baldy in a long time. Instantly, I was back in grade one when Terry nicknamed me "Baldy." It all stemmed from an episode at my cousin Bernie Marchuk's house. Bernie's dad owned the Little Muddy Water Hotel, and they lived on the second floor in a three-bedroom flat. Bernie and I were in his bedroom with the door closed, trading baseball cards. I cheered for the Dodgers, and Larry was a New York Yankees fan.

"I'll trade you a Duke Snider card for your Yogi Berra card," Bernie offered.

"The Yankees and Yogi Berra suck," I teased.

"No, they don't. The Yankees are a lot better team than your Dodgers, and Yogi Berra is the best catcher in baseball."

"No, he's not, and the Yankees suck."

Without warning, Bernie lost his cool and took a swing, hitting me on the side of my head. I reacted without thinking and slapped him hard on his cheek. Bernie began to wail, and tears flooded his eyes and rolled down his face. Not wanting his mother, who was vacuuming in the living room, to hear Bernie crying, I picked up a pair of scissors and clipped out a chunk of my hair. Bernie was still crying, so I did it again. This time he stopped crying and began to laugh. The next thing I knew, we were playing barber.

When I got home, my dad was in the living room, reading a book. I tried to sneak past him and into my bedroom, but he saw me from the corner of his eye. He looked up and asked, "Where have you been all afternoon, David?"

"Playing over at Bernie's house," I said.

Before I could leave, he asked, "What happened to your hair?"

Not knowing what to say, I blurted out, "The wind blew it off."

My dad began to laugh so hard that he doubled over, and tears filled his eyes. When he finally could speak, he said, "C'mon now, David, tell me the truth."

After I told him what had happened, he marched me into the kitchen and sat me on a stool. He opened a drawer, pulled out his clippers, and began to clip away. When he finished, my dad gave me a mirror. I couldn't believe my eyes. All my hair was gone, and I was balder than a bowling ball.

"Oh, no," I moaned in a state of shock. "I can't go to class. All the kids will laugh at me."

"Sorry, David, I had no choice. There was no way I could fix the mess you and Bernie created."

"Please, Dad," I begged, "can I stay home from school next week? It's the last week before summer vacation."

"Sorry, David, you've got to go to school. It's only a week, and you'll have all summer for your hair to grow back."

On Monday morning, I went to school wearing my Dodgers baseball cap. When I sat in my seat, I left my hat on.

"Good morning, class," Miss Stevens said.

"Good morning, Miss Stevens," we all said.

"David, please remove your cap."

"Sorry, Miss Stevens, I can't."

"And why not?"

"I just can't."

"David, remove your cap immediately, or I'll send you to the principal's office for disobedience."

Reluctantly, I took my cap off.

The uproar was instantaneous and loud.

"Oh, my God. What happened to your hair, David?" Miss Stevens asked.

"Would you believe the wind blew it off?" I said as I sank lower in my seat, my face on fire.

Once more, the class roared with laughter.

Seeing my embarrassment, Miss Stevens smiled and said, "It's okay, David, you can put your cap back on."

From the back of the room, I heard the unmistakable voice of Terry Toy yell out, "The wind blew it off. That's a good one. Hey, 'Baldy,' put your hat back on before you blind us all."

After Terry had left, Chookie picked up the can of worms and dumped them into the river. Suddenly, a giant northern pike surfaced and devoured them instantly, and the Fish flapped his tail and disappeared.

With a startled look, Chookie said, "Boy, I'm lucky I didn't jump in to search for my fishin' rod. That big fellow might have had me for lunch."

"Yeah, you're lucky you didn't jump in," I said. "I'm going to talk to Wally. See you later."

"See you, Butch."

When I got to Wally's house, he sat on the front porch strumming his acoustic guitar.

"What's up?" he said as I sat on the chair beside him.

"I just talked to Chookie, and he's in for the haunted house adventure if you'll join us." I decided not to mention our encounter with Terry Toy.

"Are you sure?"

"That's what he said."

"I don't know. The thought of that place scares the heck out of me."

"There's no reason to be afraid. We're the Three Musketeers. All for one and one for all."

Wally laughed. "Yeah, we're the Three Musketeers, all right. I'd feel safer if we had their swords to take with us."

"Don't be a chicken. Are you coming or what?"

Wally hesitated, then said, "Yeah, I guess. If Chookie's goin', I'll go. When do you think we should go?"

"How about Saturday night?"

"Okay."

"We can meet at my house tomorrow morning at ten, then go to the hideout to make plans."

"See you in the morning."

I left Wally's house whistling—happy as a chipmunk who had just found an acorn.

CHAPTER 2

The Hideout

I had difficulty falling asleep when I went to bed on Thursday evening. Visions of the house on River Road kept flashing in my head. I saw the empty rocking chair on the front veranda moving back and forth. When I finally fell asleep, I had a nightmare of the Headless Horseman dressed in black running around with an axe yelling, "Come out, come out where ever you are." In the dream, I was hiding under a bed, frozen with fear. Just as the Headless Horseman entered the room, my alarm clock shrilled and scared me half to death. I turned off the alarm. It was 7:00 a.m. I crawled out of bed, scared and excited, in a cold sweat and out of breath from my panic. Friday had finally arrived. Today Fish, Chookie, and I would head to our secret hideout, a long-abandoned shell of an old trapper's log cabin in the woods a few miles outside town. Our mission was to plan our sleepover at the so-called haunted house on River Road. Would we see a ghost or some other scary creature? Would the Headless Horseman from my dream be there? I wasn't sure I wanted to find out, but I couldn't back out now. After all, the sleepover was my bright idea.

After breakfast, I played fetch with my dog, Barney. The first day I saw Barney, he sat across the street from my dad's general store. The mangy mutt would sit for hours near the weigh scale as farmers came and went with wagons filled with grain, hay, wood, and other things that needed weighing. For some unknown reason, Barney, who looked like a Scottish terrier, loved horses. Since no one knew who he belonged to, our family adopted him and named him Barney.

Wally and Chookie showed up at ten. For a change, they were on time. We arrived at the hideout a few minutes before eleven. The cabin backed onto a small creek near a limestone quarry. It was where we played War Games, Robin Hood, Cowboys, and Indians and shot at tin cans with our slingshots. As I opened the door, a loud hiss made us all jump. Three masked bandits came running out of the cabin—a mother and two baby raccoons.

"Holy cow," Chookie shouted. "They nearly scared me half to death."

"Me, too," Wally said. "Lucky for us, they weren't skunks."

"You got that right," I said.

We all had a good laugh before cautiously venturing inside. We placed our canvas bags on the wobbly wooden table and sat in chairs we brought to the cabin last summer.

"Before our meeting," Chookie said, "I'm hungry." He opened his bag and pulled out a ham sandwich and a bottle of Coke.

"I could use some food," Wally chimed in. He dug into his bag and grabbed a banana, an apple, two oatmeal cookies, and a Pepsi.

"You on a diet, Wally?" I asked.

"Sort of," he said. "I slept in and didn't have time to make a sandwich, so I brought what I could find."

I laughed, then removed a roast beef sandwich and a carton of chocolate milk and placed them on the table.

As we snacked, I asked, "What time should we meet tomorrow night?"

"I sure don't wanna go into that spooky place after dark. Why don't we meet out front at eight? It'll still be light for almost two hours," Wally said.

"Good idea," Chookie agreed. "It's better if we go in while it's still daylight."

"Okay," I said. "I've put together a list of things we should bring." I handed them each a copy. "Take a look and let me know if I've missed anything."

Chookie began to read out loud. "Sleeping bag, pillow, flashlight, food, and drinks. I can't think of anythin' else."

Wally laughed. "I think we should all wear running shoes just in case we have to run for our lives."

"Good idea, Wally," Chookie said. "I just got a new pair of Track Stars, and I'll be sure to wear 'em."

"I don't want to scare you guys, but I had a bad dream last night. I hope it's not an omen of things to come." I went on to tell them about the Headless Horseman.

After I had finished my nightmare story, Wally said, "Geez, Butch, I was scared before you told us about your dream. Now I'm havin' second thoughts about goin' into that spooky house."

"Don't be silly," I said. "It was only a dream, and there's nothing to be frightened about."

Chookie let out a nervous laugh. "Yeah, Wally, it was only a dream. Unless Butch's dream comes true."

"That's...that's not funny, Chookie," Wally stammered.

"Let's not think about tomorrow night," I said. "Why don't we go back to town and swim at the beach?"

"Good idea," Chookie said.

"I'm game," Wally said enthusiastically.

We spent the afternoon at the beach. At six-thirty, I phoned Wally and Chookie and asked if they wanted to see the new Gene Autrey movie *The Blazing Sun*. I told them the show started at seven, so they'd better hurry. They agreed, and we met outside the theater at 6:55 p.m.

"You boys are in luck," Mr. Coffee, the owner, said. "These are the last three tickets available."

As I searched the theater for our seats, I saw Sion Johansen, the pretty blonde girl I had a crush on. She was sitting in a middle row with her brother Ernie and her two sisters Sandra and Rosalee. She smiled and waved. I grinned and waved back—one of these days, I'd build up the courage to ask her out. Terry Toy had lied and didn't have a date with Sion to see the movie. That made me feel better. As I continued to scan the theater, I spotted three empty seats in the second row from the top. I did a double-take. "Oh, no," I groaned to Wally and Chookie when I saw Terrible Terry sitting behind our seats with his bully friends, Billy Laidlaw and Peter Flett.

We sat down just as the Popeye cartoon came on the screen. I felt a kick from behind, and the unmistakable voice of Terry Toy laughed and said, "Well, if it isn't the Three Stooges, Bones, Chunky, and Walrus."

I turned around and said, "What happened to your big date with Sion Johansen?"

"I was tryin' to get you goin', Bones. Enjoy the movie."

We didn't enjoy the movie because the three bullies continued to bug us for the next two hours. I was glad when the show ended and we could leave.

CHAPTER 3

The Adventure Begins

Saturday after supper, with my hockey equipment bag, slung over my shoulder, I was ready for a night of adventure.

My mother kissed me, hugged me, and said, "Have fun sleeping over at Chookie's."

"Thanks, Mom, I'm sure I will."

From the living room, my dad yelled, "Have fun, David."

"Thanks, Dad. See you tomorrow."

I checked my watch when I arrived at the house on River Road. It was 7:51 p.m., and there was no sign of Chookie or Wally. Eight o'clock came and went, and they still weren't there. I wondered if they had chickened out after hearing my Headless Horseman nightmare story. While killing time, I discovered the back door leading into the kitchen was unlocked. At eight-fifteen, I was losing patience when I spotted Wally and Chookie strolling up the driveway toward me.

"You're late," I scolded, pointing at my watch.

"Sorry," Chookie said. "We had a late supper."

"What about you, Wally?" I asked. "What's your excuse?"

"I was listening to Amos and Andy on the radio and lost track of time."

"I thought maybe you guys had chickened out after hearing my Headless Horseman story."

"Just lookin' at this place gives me the creeps," Chookie said.

"Me, too," Wally agreed. "How are we gettin' in?"

"While I was waiting for you guys, I went around back. The door to the kitchen is unlocked."

"That's weird," Wally said. "Do you think someone's in the house?"

"Nah, you worry too much," I said, picking up my bag and walking. Chookie and Wally were right on my heels. When I opened the door, a foul, musty smell greeted us as we entered the kitchen. We turned and rushed outside, trying not to bring up our supper.

A few deep breaths later, Chookie said, "That's an awful smell. How are we goin' to sleep in there?"

"If I have to go back inside, I'm goin' to throw up for sure," Wally said as he gulped in the fresh air.

After inhaling and exhaling several times, I felt better. "No worries," I said, "I came prepared." I reached into my bag, pulled out a jar of Vicks Vapo Rub, and applied some in each nostril. I handed the jar to Chookie, and after he and Wally did the same, we were ready to go. I led the way through the dusty, cobweb-filled kitchen down the hall and into the living room. The Vicks seemed to be working. The furniture was covered by what had once been white sheets, and a few years of dust had made the covers look gray. Cobwebs hung from light fixtures and clung to the ceiling and walls.

"Let's open a few windows," I said. "Fresh air might help get rid of some of the smell."

After opening four windows, the fresh air from a gentle breeze made the house smell much better.

"I don't think I wanna spend the night in this dump," Wally said.

"Me neither," Chookie agreed.

"With a little work, it won't be so bad," I said.

I spotted an old corn broom lying on the floor. I put down my bag and began to sweep. Five minutes later, the living room looked much better.

"We can spread out our sleeping bags on the area I swept. It's plenty big enough."

"I don't know," Wally grumbled.

"Come on, guys, where's your sense of adventure?" I asked. "Are we the Three Musketeers, or what?"

"Okay," Chookie said, pulling out his sleeping bag and spreading it on the floor. Wally and I did the same.

Sitting on our sleeping bags cross-legged, I asked, "Do you want to explore the rest of the house before it gets dark?"

"I don't know," Wally said, not looking too brave.

"If we're gonna do it," Chookie said, "it's better to do it now."

"I agree," I said. "Let's go."

I stood up and headed for the stairs. The steps were firm, but the railing wobbled when I touched it.

"Be careful," I cautioned. "The stairs are okay, but the railing is a little wobbly."

When we reached the second floor, I asked, "Where do you want to start?"

"I don't care," Wally said, "as long as we stick together."

"Okay, follow me," I said. I turned to my left and headed down the hall to the first door on my right.

As I turned the knob and pushed the door open, the loud creak from rusty hinges made us jump.

Chookie said, "That noise scared me. I guess my nerves are on edge."

"Me, too," Wally whispered, letting out a nervous laugh.

The first two bedrooms were empty. The last bedroom was the largest, containing an old metal bed, a chest of drawers, and a dresser with a broken mirror. Suddenly, our heads were almost hit by two dive bombers.

"Bats!" Wally screamed. He turned quickly, bumping into Chookie.

Chookie lost his balance and fell backward onto the floor. Luckily, he wasn't hurt. He quickly jumped to his feet and followed Wally out the door.

"Hey," I said, "there's nothing to fear. Bats won't hurt you."

"Bats can get tangled up in your hair," Wally said, covering his head with his hands.

"Not true," I said. "That's an old wives' tale."

"I don't care if it's an old wives' tale. Let's get the heck outta here," Chookie said.

Wally and Chookie made a mad dash for the stairs and returned to the living room in a flash.

After exploring the room with my flashlight and finding nothing exciting, I joined my friends. They sat on their sleeping bags, eating potato chips and drinking sodas.

"My God, you two are jumpy," I said.

"This place gives me the creeps," Wally said with a shudder. "I wanna go home."

Chookie agreed. "I don't know if I can sleep here. I prefer my bed."

"Where's your sense of adventure? Don't chicken out on me now, guys. I'll never let you live it down if you go home. Besides, we haven't explored the basement or the attic," I said.

"I don't think I wanna do any more explorin'," Wally said. "I'm happy to stay right here."

"Me either," Chookie agreed.

"Okay, you two babies, promise me you'll stay here. I'm going to check the basement." I laughed. "If I don't return, send a search party."

"That's not funny," Wally said.

"If you don't return, I won't look for you, Butch. I'm runnin' outta here as fast as I can. I'll send old man Tindell to find you," Chookie said.

"Relax, nothing's going to happen to me. Just promise you'll be here when I return."

After Wally and Chookie promised not to desert me, I picked up the broom for protection and headed for the basement. When I opened the door, I was surprised it didn't squeak. I pointed my flashlight at the steps. They looked solid, and I was sure they could support a lightweight like me. As I descended into the dark unknown, a shiver of fear crept down my spine, and my heart began to race. Reaching the bottom, I wasn't surprised to find a dirt floor. A damp, musty smell hung in the stale air. As I circled the basement with my flashlight, I could see cobwebs everywhere. On the far wall, I spotted a wooden workbench. I decided to go and take a look. When I shone my light on the bench, it was empty except for a claw hammer. The hammerhead appeared to be covered with a dark substance. Was it blood, or was it paint? I jumped when I felt something brush against my leg. Shining the light on the floor, I saw a brown rat scurry across the room. The rodent ran through an open door and disappeared into the cold room. With my heart in my throat, I ran up the stairs to tell my friends about the hammer. When I reached the living room, Chookie and Wally were snuggled up in their sleeping bags, snoring. I checked my watch. It was almost ten. I was hungry, so I ate an oatmeal cookie and then crawled into my sleeping bag, and within minutes I was out like a light.

I wasn't sure if I was awake or dreaming. Floating above me, I could see the spirit of an elderly woman. Who was she, and what did she want?

"Check the attic, David. I'm in the attic."

In a blink of an eye, she vanished into thin air.

I lay there as if in a trance staring at the ceiling. Was what I saw real, or was my mind playing tricks on me? I decided not to wake up Wally and Chookie. The story would either scare them to death or cause them to laugh at me and my wild imagination. I chalked the vision up to my mind playing tricks on me. A minute later, I rolled over and went back to sleep.

I was jarred awake by a loud crash of thunder. Startled, I sat up just as a blinding flash of lightning lit up the room for a split second. A howling wind shook the house, and a heavy rain drummed loudly on the metal roof. I checked my watch—it was almost midnight.

Wouldn't you know, I thought, *a sleepover in a haunted house wouldn't be complete without a thunderstorm at the bewitching hour.*

I glanced at Chookie and Wally, and they were still fast asleep. I rolled over and closed my eyes. I was dozing off when, between claps of thunder, I could swear that a chain began to rattle somewhere on the second floor. Clink-clank, clink-clank, clink-clank. I lay in my sleeping bag, frozen with fear. A few seconds later, the thump of heavy footsteps echoed from the stairway, and the rattling chain grew louder.

A booming voice echoed, "Beware! I'm coming to get you," followed by a bone-chilling laugh.

"Wally, Chookie," I yelled. "Wake up."

My panicked voice startled them. Wally and Chookie sat up instantly. Still half asleep, rubbing his eyes, Wally mumbled, "What is it? What's happening?"

Not remembering where he was, Chookie seemed disoriented. As his mind cleared, he asked, "What's going on, Butch?"

Before I could answer, a flash of lightning lit up the room. A scary creature stood in the doorway. Dressed in black, holding a two-sided axe in one hand and a chain in the other, the menacing figure blocked our escape route. My dream had come true, and I stared in disbelief at the Headless Horseman.

The Horseman dropped the chain and raised the axe above his headless head, and growled. "It's time to meet your maker, Stooges."

"Please, Mr. Horseman," Chookie pleaded. "Don't hurt us. We're just kids."

Wally opened his mouth to speak, but nothing came out.

Suddenly it hit me. The Headless Horseman was Terrible Terry Toy.

"Nice try, T.T.," I said. "I know it's you."

"And how would you know that?" the Horseman asked.

"Because you're the only idiot who calls us Stooges," I said.

That's when Wally found his tongue. "Yeah, T.T., we know it's you."

Terry began to laugh. "Had you goin' there for a minute, didn't I, Stooges?"

"Yeah, you did," I said. "How'd you know we'd be here?"

Pulling off his costume, Terry said, "I followed you idiots to the old trapper cabin yesterday and overheard your plans. Your story about the Headless Horseman dream gave me the idea, so I decided to have fun with you, Stooges."

"What you did was really funny, T.T.," I said sarcastically.

"I'm glad you enjoyed it, Bones. I wanted to scare the hell out of you guys. Did I succeed?"

"Yeah, you did," Wally said. "I almost messed my pants."

"Me, too," Chookie said. "I thought for sure we were all gonna die."

"Where did you get the costume?" I asked.

"It belongs to my older brother, Rickey. My mom made it for him for Halloween two years ago."

"When you got here, was the back door unlocked?" I asked.

"I got here around seven. The back door was locked, but I brought some keys from my dad's workshop. I tried several before one of the skeleton keys worked. Get it. Skeleton key, haunted house." Terry laughed at his stupid joke, and so did we. "I hid in the closet in the large bedroom. I put my costume on before midnight, and you know the rest. I'm dyin' of thirst. Anyone got a drink?"

"Sure," I said. I pulled out a Coke and tossed it to Terry.

"Thanks," he said.

"You're welcome," I said.

For the first time, I could remember, Terry and I were civil to one another.

"So, have you seen any ghosts yet?" T.T. asked with a laugh.

"I think I did," I said. I told the story of my vision of the old lady who had hovered above my head telling me to check out the attic.

When I finished the story, Wally said, "You won't catch me goin' into the attic in this house."

"Me neither," Chookie said.

"I'll go with you, Bones," Terry said, trying to sound brave. "These two chickens can stay here and lay eggs. Just in case we run into a monster or somethin', I'd better take the axe with us," T.T. said.

"Good idea," I said as we headed for the second floor.

The stairs to the attic were at the end of the hallway.

"You go first, Bones," Terry said.

"Okay," I said, shining my flashlight on the steps.

Once I was inside, I did a quick survey with my flashlight. Like every room in the house, the attic was filled with cobwebs and dust. Cardboard boxes were piled everywhere. I opened a box with pictures, junk, and antiques from another era. Two old wicker chairs sat in the middle of the room, and a single bed sat against the far wall. Something on the mattress bulged under a tattered sheet. Curious, I went over to the bed and pulled back the sheet. What I saw in the beam of light made my stomach flip and my heart pound with fear. My body went numb as I stared down at a human skeleton. There were two holes on the back of the skull, each about the size of a quarter. Could the hammer I found on the workbench have caused these holes? Were these bones the remains of Mrs. Crookshank?

Suddenly, hovering above the bed, I saw the same spirit, ghost, or whatever I had encountered in the living room earlier that night.

"Thank you for coming, David. You are a brave boy. Please tell the authorities that I was murdered by my husband, Clarence Crookshank, and he killed me in a fit of rage with a hammer. When I am finally laid to rest, my spirit will be free to leave this hell on earth and go to the other side where I belong."

Before I could speak, the spirit of Mrs. Crookshank vanished.

"Terry, did you see that?" I asked, half excited, half scared.

When I turned around, the door was closed, and there was no sign of Terry. I tried to open the door, but it was locked.

"What the…Terry," I screamed, "That's not funny."

"See ya, Bones," Terry yelled back. "Have fun in the attic."

"Terry. Don't leave. Open the door."

No reply. Terry was gone.

I kicked and kicked, but the door wouldn't open. I yelled at the top of my lungs for several minutes, but Chookie and Wally couldn't hear me. The howling wind, booming thunder, and pounding rain drowned out my desperate calls for help. Exhausted and scared, I sat down on the floor and cried. That's when I realized that I was locked in the attic with the skeleton and spirit of Mrs. Crookshank. Would I ever get out? Would I die here?

It took a few minutes of deep breathing before I calmed down and cleared the negative thoughts from my mind. I was physically and mentally exhausted, and I needed to sleep. I got up and rummaged through several boxes until I found a blanket and a pillow. I shook the dust out of the blanket, spread it on the floor, and lay down. As soon as my head hit the pillow, I was fast asleep.

Thump, thump, thump. "Butch, Terry, are you in there?" Chookie yelled.

For a minute, I thought I was dreaming. I sat up and listened. My watch showed 8:10 a.m.

Thump, thump, thump. "Hey, are you guys in there?" Wally's voice this time.

I jumped up and thumped back on the attic door. "Help! I'm locked in here by myself. Get me out."

Seconds later, the door opened. Chookie stood on the ladder with a big grin on his face.

"Thanks, Chookie," I said with a sigh of relief.

When Chookie and I were back in the hallway, Wally asked, "Where's Terry?"

"I don't know," I said. "After locking me in the attic, the idiot must have taken off."

"You couldn't get out," Chookie said, "because Terry locked the deadbolt."

"No wonder it wouldn't open," I said. "Let's go back to the living room. Boy, have I got a story to tell you guys."

The storm was finally over, and the house was as quiet as a morgue. As we sat on our sleeping bags, a ray of sunlight managed to pierce the grime-filled windows and light up the room.

"Are you ready?" I asked.

Chookie and Fish nodded, and I began. When I finished the story, they sat briefly in stunned silence.

Finally, Chookie said, "So it's true, the ghost of Mrs. Crookshank haunts the house."

"Wow," Wally said. "Is Mrs. Crookshank a friendly ghost, like Casper?"

"I don't know. I think so," I said. "It's time to get out of here and see Constable Tindell."

"Do you think he'll believe you, Butch?" Chookie asked.

"Probably not, but I've got to try."

At first, Constable Tindell didn't believe my story. He said that I had a wild imagination. I wouldn't leave the police station until he finally agreed to go to the house and check it out. A few days later, dental records proved that the remains found in the attic were those of Mrs. Crookshank.

My dad was slightly annoyed that I had disobeyed his warning to stay away from the house on River Road. However, he was pleased I had found the remains of Mrs. Crookshank, and the mystery of her disappearance was finally solved.

The day Mrs. Crookshank was laid to rest, Father John, the local Catholic priest, and an elderly couple were the only people at her graveside. I hid behind a tree and watched as the priest said a few prayers and blessed the coffin. After Father John and the older couple had left, two workers lowered the casket into the ground and began filling the hole with dirt. When the job was completed, the workers got into a truck and drove away. As I was leaving, I looked at Mrs. Crookshank's grave. That's when I saw Mrs. Crookshank's spirit rise from the ground. She smiled at me, waved goodbye, and disappeared into the clear blue sky. She was finally free from her earthly hell. Mrs. Crookshank had gone to the other side, and I believe she is now at peace in heaven with the Lord.

The stranger

I was sitting on a chair in my dad's general store munching on a Sweet Marie chocolate bar when a tall, slim stranger wearing mirrored sunglasses came through the door. He was dressed entirely in black. Despite the hot weather, he wore black pants, a black shirt, a black top hat, highly polished black shoes, and a long black trench coat. Snow-white hair hung below his hat, his skin was chalk-white, and his beak-like nose reminded me of a bird. He strolled up to the counter where my dad had just finished serving a customer and said, "Good morning, my name is Bonaparte Blackbird. Please excuse me for not removing my sunglasses, sir, as my eyes are susceptible to light."

"No problem, Mr. Blackbird, I understand. I'm Bill Fairburn. How may I help you?"

"I'm interested in purchasing a house in your town. The one on River Road."

"I see. Are you aware the house is scheduled to be demolished next week?"

"I wasn't aware of that, sir. Who is in charge of the property?"

"The village of Little Muddy Water owns the property. It was legally acquired for back taxes owed after the owner, Clarence Crookshank, passed away. I suggest you speak to our mayor, Mr. Victor Wamsley, at the town hall."

"And how would I get to your town hall, sir?"

"Go out the door and turn left. The town hall is two blocks down Main Street."

"Thank you for your help, Mr. Fairburn."

"My pleasure, Mr. Blackbird. Have a nice day."

"You too, sir."

The mayor's secretary, Lisa Carter, pretended not to notice the appearance of the unusual-looking man as she ushered Bonaparte Blackbird into the mayor's office. He sat and waited until the mayor had finished signing some papers. When Mayor Wamsley looked up, he was surprised to see a weird-looking man with mirrored sunglasses staring at him.

"Good day, sir. I'm Mayor Victor Wamsley." The mayor extended his hand, and the two men shook hands.

"Pleased to meet you, Mr. Mayor. I'm Bonaparte Blackbird."

"How can I help you, Mr. Blackbird?" the mayor asked.

"I would like to purchase the house on River Road."

That wasn't what the mayor was expecting to hear. He paused momentarily before saying, "We plan to demolish the house next week, but the land will be for sale."

"I'm sorry, Mr. Mayor, I didn't make myself clear. I wish to purchase the property with the house intact, and there will be no need to demolish it, sir."

"I'm sure that can be arranged, Mr. Blackbird."

After agreeing to an all-cash purchase price, the mayor said, "I will present your offer this evening at our council meeting and let you know their decision first thing in the morning. How can I get in touch with you, Mr. Blackbird?"

"I'm staying at the Little Muddy Water Hotel. Why don't I stop by your office at ten tomorrow morning?"

"That would be fine, Mr. Blackbird. I look forward to giving you good news in the morning."

They shook hands, and Blackbird left.

At 10:00 a.m. the following morning, Bonaparte Blackbird met with Mayor Wamsley. The mayor greeted him with a welcoming smile and said, "Mr. Blackbird, I'm pleased to inform you that the council approved your offer to purchase the house on River Road."

"That's great news, Mr. Mayor. I'm looking forward to becoming a resident of your beautiful village."

"If you don't mind me asking, Mr. Blackbird, where will you move from?"

"Currently, I live in Muddy Water. I recently sold my business and decided to retire to a small community where I could relax and enjoy life. I'm sick and tired of the hustle and bustle of big city living."

"I'm curious, Mr. Blackbird, what business were you in?"

"I owned a funeral home. I'm a mortician. The business was 'dead,' but I earned a lot of money," Blackbird said, laughing at his bad joke

Mayor Wamsley chuckled at Blackbird's attempt at humor. He stood up and extended his hand. After shaking hands, he said, "Welcome to Little Muddy Water. I hope your move goes smoothly. It's been a pleasure meeting you, Mr. Blackbird."

"It was a pleasure meeting you, Mr. Mayor. Have a pleasant day.""

The Coffin

Chookie, Fish, and I were on our way to our hideout to hang out and play games. As we approached the house on River Road, a long, black car stopped at the driveway entrance. At first, I thought the vehicle was a limousine, but after a second glance, I realized the car was an old hearse. The driver got out and said, "Hey, boys, my name is Blackbird, Bonaparte Blackbird, the new owner of this beautiful house. How would you like to earn five bucks each?"

I recognized Mr. Blackbird. He was the same weird-looking man who came into my dad's store a few weeks ago. Mirrored sunglasses hid his eyes, and he wore the same black clothes, including the long black trench coat.

"What would we have to do?" I asked.

"Not much. I need a hand moving something into my new home," he said. "It'll only take a few minutes."

"Sure," Chookie said enthusiastically. "I could use an extra five dollars. It'll help pay for my new fishing rod."

"I'm game," Wally said.

"Okay," I said.

"Good," Blackbird said. "Just follow the car."

Blackbird parked near the front entrance, went to the back of the hearse, and opened the rear door. He bent over and pulled a gleaming oak coffin halfway out. He pointed and said, "You three take hold of the handle on that side, and I'll get this side." He gave an amused smile as if reading our minds. "Don't worry. It's empty.

The three of us glanced at one another with puzzled looks, but no one said a word. We carried the coffin into the house and set it down on the living room floor as instructed by Mr. Blackbird. He put a hand into his pocket and pulled out a stack of money. He peeled off three five-dollar bills and handed one to each of us. "Thanks. I appreciate your help, boys. By the way, what are your names?"

"I'm David, and these are my friends Marvin and Wally."

"Pleased to meet you, David, Marvin, and Wally."

I boldly asked, "What is the coffin for, Mr. Blackbird?"

"It's for me." Reading my confused look, he smiled and said, "For when I die."

"Oh," I said.

"Are you going to die soon?" Wally asked.

Blackbird laughed. "I hope not."

"Why are you wearing a heavy coat on such a hot day?" I asked.

Once more, Blackbird laughed and said, "I'm an albino, and I have a condition called albinism. Albinism makes my hair and skin very white and my eyes sensitive to sunlight. That's why I wear sunglasses. I wear a coat because my thyroid gland is out of whack. I call the condition North Pole syndrome. I feel like I'm freezing all the time."

"Oh," I said, not understanding what Mr. Blackbird had just said.

"Do you wear your sunglasses at night?" Wally asked.

"No, son, I can see quite well in the dark."

"Where are you from, Mr. Blackbird?" I asked.

"I was born in Transylvania but moved to this country thirty years ago. I've lived in Muddy Water until now."

"I read that vampires live in Transylvania," I said. "Are you a vampire? Do you know Dracula?"

Once more, Blackbird laughed. "No, I'm not a vampire and don't know Dracula. I'm a retired mortician, and I owned a funeral home."

"What's a mortician?" Wally asked.

"A mortician is a person who prepares the body of a deceased person for private or public viewing. To do this, I have to drain the blood from the body and then use a chemical to embalm the body."

"Why do you drain the blood and embalm a dead person?" I asked.

"Draining the blood and embalming the body prevents decomposition so that the body won't stink when people view it."

"Why are you moving here?" Chookie asked.

Bonaparte Blackbird smiled and said, "You sure are a curious lot, aren't you? To answer your question, I sold my business and moved here to relax and escape the stress of big city life."

Chookie gave Wally and me a look that said *enough questions, let's get out of here.* And that's what we did, and we barely spoke until we reached our hideout.

As we sat at the table eating chips and drinking sodas, I asked, "Is Mr. Blackbird weird, or what?"

"Yeah," Chookie said, "He's weird, and he gives me the creeps."

"He scares me more than the haunted house," Wally said.

"I agree. There's something about Mr. Blackbird that's not right, and I think he's hiding something," I said.

"What do you think he's hidin'?" Chookie asked.

"I don't know," I replied.

"Maybe he's a vampire," Fish said, his eyes growing wider.

"You could be right," Chookie said. "He drains blood from dead people, and maybe he sleeps in his coffin."

"Yeah, I bet he sleeps in his coffin during the day and stalks his victims at night. Boo!" I yelled.

Fish and Chookie both jumped.

"That's not funny, Butch," Wally said.

"Yeah, Butch. Are you tryin' to give me a heart attack?" Chookie said, punching me on the arm.

"Come on, guys, get a grip," I said. "Wanna hear a vampire joke?"

"Not if it's scary," Fish said.

"It's not scary."

"Okay," Chookie said. "Promise it's not scary."

"I promise. What did the vampire say to the person who did him a favor?"

"I don't have a clue," Fish said.

"Me neither," Chookie said.

"Fangs a lot."

"That's corny," Wally said, but we all laughed.

"Let's forget about vampires and Mr. Blackbird. Let's go outside and shoot cans with our slingshots," I said.

We placed a tin can on a stump. From thirty feet away, we took turns trying to knock it over. Chookie ended up as champ for the day. He had eight hits out of ten tries, I had seven, and Fish had only five. After the contest, we played hide-and-seek for another hour, called it a day, and headed home.

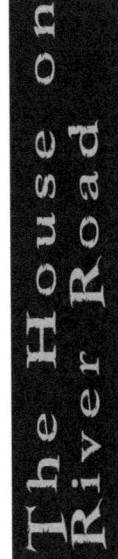

Mischief

When I went to bed that night, it took a while for me to fall asleep. The vision of Mr. Blackbird and his coffin kept flashing through my head. I wondered if he was really from Transylvania and if he was a vampire.

The next morning, after breakfast, I called on Chookie.

"What do you want to do today?" I asked.

"I don't know. Why don't we call on Fish and see if he has any ideas?"

"Okay," I said, and we headed to Wally's house.

Fish was finishing breakfast when we arrived, so we waited on the front porch. Five minutes later, he appeared and asked, "What's up, guys?"

"We don't know what we want to do today. Do you have any ideas?" I asked.

"Yeah, I do. Why don't we go to the stockyard and ride sheep?" Fish suggested.

"Great idea," Chookie said.

"Sounds good to me," I said. "Let's go."

The stockyard was full of sheep, pigs, and cattle when we arrived.

"The ground looks muddy," Fish said. "I forgot that it rained last night."

"What do you think, Butch?" Chookie asked.

"We're here now. Let's not let a little mud spoil our fun." I said. "Besides, the mud will wash off."

By the time we finished, all three of us were covered in mud from head to toe and reeked from sheep manure.

When I got home, I went to the backyard and pumped a pail full of water from the well. I found a rag and began to wash off the mud, which had already dried. My mother came onto the landing at the top of the stairs to shake out a mat and spotted me. "David," she yelled, "what are you doing?"

"Washing off mud," I said.

My mother ran down the stairs. In a demanding voice, she asked, "And where did you get mud on your clothes?"

Sheepishly, I said, "At the stockyard riding sheep."

"My God, you smell awful. Go up to the landing and remove your clothes and leave them there. Then go in and take a bath."

"Please don't tell Dad," I pleaded.

"I won't if you promise to stay away from the stockyard."

"I promise," I said as I headed up the stairs.

After supper, I met Fish and Chookie, and we headed to the river to a place called "the rocks" to catch some fish. In one hour, we had landed ten walleye.

As we headed home, I remembered the half-package of Buckingham cigarettes I had found on the sidewalk in front of my dad's store. I pulled them out of my jacket pocket, put one in my mouth, and passed one to Chookie and one to fish.

"I've never smoked before," Fish said.

"Me neither," Chookie said.

"I haven't either," I said. "Let's give it a try."

I had brought a small box of matches, and we all lit up. Puffing away as we walked through the field heading toward home, thinking we were "big shots," we tried to inhale like real smokers. It didn't take long before we felt dizzy and began to choke and cough.

As we neared her house, my Aunt Rose stormed out the back door, waving her finger. She shouted, "David Fairburn, what are you and your friends doing? I'm going to tell your parents that you were smoking."

"Please, Aunt Rose, don't tell my mom and dad. We won't smoke anymore."

We threw the cigarettes to the ground and stomped them out.

As we passed by, with our heads bowed, Aunt Rose stood on the back porch with her hands on her hips, mumbling to herself.

Aunt Rose never told my parents. After our bad experience, I threw the remaining cigarettes away, and we all vowed never to smoke again as long as we lived.

The following day, when I went into the kitchen for breakfast, my mother asked, "David, did you and your friends leave any of the pens open at the stockyard yesterday?"

"What?" I said.

"Pardon. The word is pardon, David. Watch your manners."

"Sorry, Mom."

"Yesterday. Did you leave any of the pens open at the stockyard?"

"No. Why do you ask?"

"Go look out the front window."

I got up and went into the living room. When I peered out the window, I couldn't believe my eyes. Across the street, the field was filled with cattle, sheep, and pigs. Our dog, Barney, and another dog were barking and chasing the panicked animals around, nipping at their hoofs.

"Oh my God," I said.

My mother said, "Are you sure you had nothing to do with leaving the gates open?"

"I swear we had nothing to do with it, Mom."

Someone knocked on the door, and my mother went to see who was there. I was scared when I heard Constable Tindell's voice. "Good morning, Mrs. Fairburn. Is David home?"

"Yes, he is."

"May I speak to him, please?"

"David, Constable Tindell wishes to speak to you."

I went into the kitchen, wondering what Mr. Tindell wanted.

"Good morning, David." Constable Tindell said.

"Good morning, Constable Tindell," I said.

"I'll get right to the point. I was informed by a witness that he saw you and your friends, Walter Fisher and Marvin Morris, at the stockyard yesterday. Is that correct?"

"Yes, Constable Tindell, we were there."

"What were you doing?"

"We were playing."

"What do you mean, playing?"

I looked at the floor and mumbled, "We were riding sheep."

"Did you happen to leave any of the gates open when you left the stockyard?"

"No, Constable Tindell, we didn't. All the gates were closed when we left."

"I questioned your two friends, who told me the same story. Did you happen to see anyone else there yesterday?"

"No, Constable Tindell. We were the only ones there."

That's when my mom said, "If they had left the gates open yesterday afternoon, the animals would have been roaming around town before dark. No one spotted them until this morning. Someone opened the gates in the middle of the night, and David and his friends had nothing to do with it."

"What you're saying makes sense, Mrs. Fairburn. Sorry to have bothered you. David, do you know who might have opened the pens?"

"Sorry, Constable Tindell, I don't."

"Okay. Thank you. Goodbye, Mrs. Fairburn."

"Goodbye, Constable Tindell," my mother said.

I had no proof, but I couldn't help but think that T.T. and his bully friends may have had something to do with the animals escaping.

It took the rest of the day before all the animals could be rounded up and returned to captivity. A man with a shotgun sat in his truck. He guarded the stockyard until the following morning when several cattle trucks arrived to deliver the animals to the slaughterhouse in Muddy Water.

That same day, Chookie, Fish, and I took our slingshots and went to the old abandoned Brock Fisheries building on the river. We were breaking windows when a booming voice said, "What are you boys doing?"

Startled, we all jumped. Constable Tindell had snuck up on us, catching us in the act.

"I should arrest you all for vandalism," he said sternly.

"Sorry," I said. "I saw other kids breaking windows here a few weeks ago."

"Those kids were lucky I didn't catch them. Do you know who they were?'

I knew it was Terry Toy and a few of his friends, but I didn't want to rat them out.

"Sorry, Constable Tindell, I don't know who they were," I lied.

"I find that hard to believe," he said. "Now, get out of here before I change my mind and arrest you all. And don't let me catch you here again. Scoot."

Like three scared rabbits, we ran as fast as we could without looking back.

We decided to go to Muddy Beach Park with gloves, a bat, a few balls, and bathing suits. We took turns hitting the ball to the outfield. In the field, I pretended to be my favorite player, Duke Snider.

After a few hours of working up a sweat, we changed into our swimsuits and cooled off in the lake. Believe it or not, we didn't get into any more mischief that day.

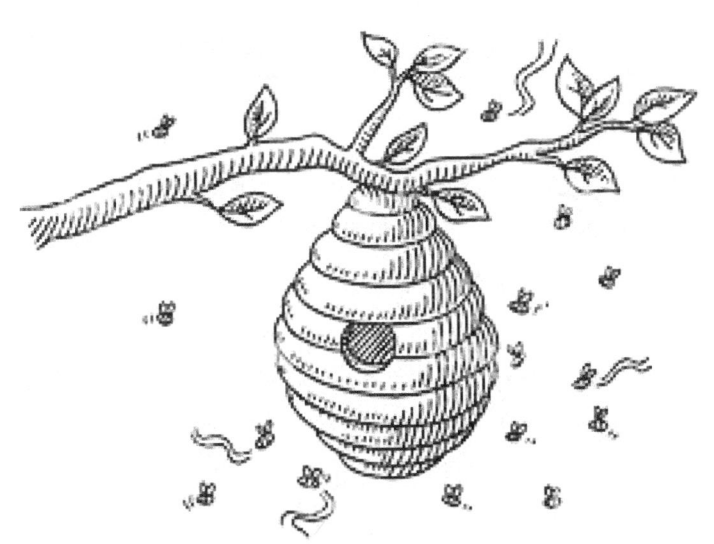

CHAPTER 7

Busy Bees

few days later, Mr. Blackbird's house was a beehive of activity. Wally, Chookie, and I were on our way to the hideout. We stopped at the driveway entrance to see what was going on. Men were replacing the metal roof, and workers were coming and going from inside the house.

"Hey, boys," Mr. Blackbird shouted as he walked toward us. "How would you like to earn some more money?"

"What would we have to do this time?" I asked.

"Deliver fliers to all the houses and businesses in town."

"What kind of fliers?" Chookie asked.

"In a few weeks, when the work on my house is completed, I'm going to have an open house."

"What's an open house?" Fish asked.

"An open house is when I invite people to come and see my house. I want to get to know the residents of Little Muddy Water, and

I think having an open house will give me that opportunity. I will be providing free food and drinks for everyone."

"An open house sounds like fun," Fish said.

"How much will you pay us to deliver your fliers?" Chookie asked.

"Does twenty dollars each sound reasonable?"

"Yes," we all said at the same time.

"Okay, come and see me two weeks from today. I'll have the fliers ready by then."

"See you in two weeks," I said.

After Blackbird returned to the house, Chookie said, "Twenty bucks will pay off the balance I owe Mr. Lemon for my new fishing rod."

Two weeks later, we went back to see Mr. Blackbird. When we arrived, he asked, "Would you boys like to see the changes to my house?"

"Sure," I said.

"As you can see, I've had the metal roofing and all the windows replaced. The house has been painted inside and out, and the veranda is fixed. I've added some shrubs and a flowerbed to the front yard, and the lawn was resodded."

Mr. Blackbird led us inside. Gray carpeting and dark brown hardwood flooring had been installed throughout most of the house. The kitchen had been updated with black ceramic tiles and dark gray cupboards. The main-floor bathroom and second-floor bathroom were decorated entirely with black fixtures. Chookie, Fish, and I were surprised to see all the walls painted in Mr. Blackbird's favorite color—black.

When we had finished the tour, Mr. Blackbird asked, "Well, what do you think, boys? Do you like it?"

We all looked at one another, not knowing what to say. We didn't want to offend Mr. Blackbird. Finally, I said, "It sure is different."

Wally and Chookie agreed. Mr. Blackbird laughed and said, "I can tell you're puzzled by my choice of colors or lack thereof. As I've already mentioned, my eyes are very susceptible to bright light, and darker colors help me see better without sunglasses."

"Oh," I said, "I forgot about that."

"Me, too," Chookie said.

"I forgot about it, too," Fish said.

Mr. Blackbird entered the kitchen and brought back three bundles of open-house fliers. He handed us each a stack. Next, he pulled out a wad of cash and gave us each a twenty-dollar bill.

"Thanks, boys. I appreciate you helping me out again. Once the front yard has new grass and the flower beds are in, how would you like to cut and trim my lawn and weed the flower beds every Saturday until summer is over? I'll pay you five dollars each every Saturday."

"Sure, Mr. Blackbird, we'd be glad to," I said.

Chookie and Fish agreed.

I glanced at the top leaflet of the bundle of fliers in my hands—it read:

OPEN HOUSE
666 River Road
Saturday, August 25, 1951
1:00 p.m.-5:00 p.m.
Complimentary Food & Drinks

We used our bikes. It took a little over two hours to deliver all the fliers. To cool off, we met at the beach and went swimming.

I turned eleven on August 24, the day before Mr. Blackbird's open house, and my parents surprised me with a birthday party. They invited Chookie, Fish, and a few other kids from my class, including three girls. I was surprised when Sion Johanson walked through the door.

Sion smiled and said, "Happy birthday, Butch." She gave me a present wrapped in colorful paper and a peck on the cheek.

I could feel my face flush, and I'm sure it turned redder than a beet. "Th…thanks, Sion," I managed to stammer.

When it came time to blow out the eleven candles on the chocolate birthday cake my mom had baked, I couldn't wait to open my presents. From Chookie and Fish, I received fishing lures. Sion's gift was a Monopoly game, and I received an assortment of comic books from the other kids. My last gift was from my mom and dad. It was wrapped in a box about three feet long, and I prayed it was the gift I had wanted. When I tore open the box, I was not disappointed. I couldn't believe my eyes. There it was, a brand new Daisy Red Ryder BB Gun. My prayers had been answered.

All afternoon, I couldn't take my eyes off Sion. Just before she left, I worked up the courage to ask her on a date to see a movie. She smiled and said, "I'd love to go with you, Butch." We decided to see the new Roy Rogers movie on Saturday night of the long weekend before school started. That was the happiest day of my life. I felt like I was walking on air.

Before they left my birthday party, I made arrangements to meet Chookie and Fish after supper. We headed to our hideout with our B.B. guns for some target practice. I was now an official member of the Red Ryder BB gun club.

The Open House

The village had been buzzing with curiosity and anticipation for the entire week before the Open House date. Mr. Bonaparte Blackbird was the main topic of conversation. Everyone appeared anxious to meet the strange new resident of Little Muddy Water.

On August 25 at 12:30 p.m., a lineup began forming outside the house on River Road. At 1:00 p.m., the front door opened, and Bonaparte Blackbird stepped out onto the veranda. He wore mirrored sunglasses, a black business suit, a black shirt, and a black tie.

Blackbird smiled and said, "Thank you for coming. I'm looking forward to meeting each of you in person. Please come in."

Ladies in black uniforms with hors d'oeuvres and champagne trays greeted guests as they arrived. Other ladies served soda pop, peanut butter, and jam sandwiches for the children, and two bartenders served beer and mixed drinks in the living room. At first, most people were shocked to see the dark interior, but when

Blackbird explained the reason, everyone relaxed and enjoyed the friendly atmosphere.

I watched Mr. Blackbird play the perfect host, smiling and shaking hands with everyone. After meeting and speaking to every guest, Mr. Blackbird went to the bar and returned to where I stood with my mom and dad. He held a tall glass filled with a red liquid. Curious, I asked, "Mr. Blackbird, what are you drinking?"

He smiled and said, "What I'm drinking, David, is called a Bloody Mary."

"Oh," I said. "Is there blood in a Bloody Mary?"

Blackbird laughed and said, "No, David, there isn't any blood in a Bloody Mary. The drink is made with vodka and tomato juice, salt is put around the rim, and a celery stick is placed inside the glass."

"That sounds like a weird drink to me, Mr. Blackbird."

"David," my dad scolded. "Mind your manners."

"Sorry, Dad. Sorry, Mr. Blackbird."

Blackbird laughed. "No problem, Mr. Fairburn. I enjoy the curiosity of children. By asking questions, that's how they learn."

After Blackbird had moved on, I asked my dad, "What are you eating, Dad?"

"They're a delicacy called escargots, David."

"What are they?"

"Escargot is a fancy name for snail."

"Yuck," I said. "Why would you want to eat snails?"

My dad laughed. "Because they taste delicious, son. I'm also eating caviar."

"What's caviar?"

"Caviar is fish eggs."

"I think I'll stick to a peanut butter and jam sandwich," I said.

Chookie and Fish were there with their parents, and they spotted me and came over to say hello.

"Are you enjoying Mr. Blackbird's open house?" I asked.

"Yeah, it's great. All the food and drinks are free," Chookie said, stuffing a sandwich into his mouth.

"I've had three sandwiches and two sodas," Fish said. "Mr. Blackbird is a nice man."

"Yeah, he is," I agreed. "This open house must be costing him a fortune."

"It must be," Chookie said.

"Mr. Blackbird must be rich," Fish said.

"It sure looks that way," I said. "My dad told me Mr. Blackbird hired a caterer from Dolphin."

By 5:00 p.m., the last few stragglers had left the house. Everyone seemed to have enjoyed meeting the mysterious new resident of Little Muddy Water. For the next few days, the open house and Bonaparte Blackbird was the main topic of conversation.

Back to school

Going back to school made me feel sad. Summer vacation was over, and I dreaded the thought of studying and homework. The only thing that made me feel a little better, Sion, was now my girlfriend. We enjoyed the Roy Roger movie on Saturday night, and when T.T. saw us at the show, I could tell he was jealous. After the movie, I walked Sion home, and to my surprise, she kissed me goodnight.

On Tuesday morning, my head was still in a cloud as Sion and I strolled to school hand in hand. When we entered our classroom, she went and sat next to her best girlfriend, Marilyn Magnuson. I joined Chookie and Fish, and before we could start a conversation, a short, stout black woman entered the room. I thought my eyes were playing a trick on me. I had never seen a black person before, and I suspected neither had anyone else in Little Muddy Water.

"Good mornin' class," the woman said with a funny accent I had never heard before. "My name is Mrs. Kirkland. I'm your new teacher, and I'm lookin' forward to meetin' all of you."

"Good morning, Mrs. Kirkland," the class said in unison.

Mrs. Kirkland spent the rest of the morning getting to know each of her students. It was almost noon by the time she talked to us all. Just before the lunch bell rang, I asked, "Where did you come from, Mrs. Kirkland?"

She laughed and said, "I bet most of you have never seen a black person before, am I right?"

"You're right," Terry Toy shouted.

Mrs. Kirkland ignored Terry and said, "To answer your question, I'm from the United States, a city called Savannah in the state of Georgia."

"Oh," I said. "I'm sure that's far from Little Muddy Water."

"It sure is. I met my husband while he was on vacation. He was from Muddy Water. To make a long story short, I moved to your country when we decided to get married." She laughed. "When I applied for a teaching job in Little Muddy Water, I thought it was a suburb of Muddy Water. When I accepted the teaching position, I didn't realize it was 250 miles away. I was shocked when I learned I couldn't commute daily, so my husband and I moved here a week ago. We rented a house on 4th street."

Chookie asked. "Mrs. Kirkland, how come you talk funny?"

She smiled and said, "I speak with a southern drawl."

The lunch bell rang, and everyone stood up, preparing to leave. Mrs. Kirkland said, "Since this is the first day of school, you have the afternoon off. Be here at nine tomorrow mornin' prepared to crack the books. See you in the mornin'."

Mrs. Veronica Kirkland turned out to be an excellent teacher, but she didn't know much about our country. We told her white whales were in the pond at the limestone quarry, and she believed us.

Halloween

The first month of school flew by, and before I knew it, it was the last day of October. I awoke and looked out my bedroom window. I was surprised to see a light dusting of snow on the ground. It looked more like Christmas than Halloween. I thought the school day would never end. When I got home, I ate an early supper, changed into my costume, and rushed to Wally's

house. Chookie was already there. We were on another adventure, dressed as the Three Musketeers.

After knocking on doors for two hours, our pillowcases were bulging with candy, chocolate bars, and apples. Our last stop was the house on River Road. Mr. Blackbird had invited us to stop by, saying he had some "special treats" for us. All the other kids in town feared Mr. Blackbird and avoided his house like the plague. A sign on his front door read: *Welcome, boys! Please come in. Your Halloween treats are on the kitchen table.*

As we entered the front hallway, Fish said, "What kind of treats do you think Mr. Blackbird left for us?"

"I don't have a clue," Chookie said.

"There's only one way to find out," I said. "Let's go to the kitchen."

We found a handwritten note on the kitchen table and three envelopes with our names. I picked up the letter and began to read it out loud.

Dear Boys:

I want to thank you for all the help you've given me. You have been good friends in the brief time that I have known you. As a token of appreciation, I have left you each a little parting gift. It is time for me to leave earth and return to my home. Goodbye.

Sincerely,

Bonaparte Blackbird

We were shocked to find ten one-hundred-dollar bills in each envelope.

"Wow," Chookie said, his eyes wide with glee. "I can buy a lot of fishing gear with all this money, and maybe even a baseball glove and a pair of skates."

"Mr. Blackbird must be a rich man," Fish said, stuffing the money into his pocket.

"I agree. I wonder where Mr. Blackbird has gone?" I said.

"Maybe he went back to Muddy Water," Fish said.

"I don't think so," I said. "The note says Mr. Blackbird's leaving earth." Suddenly it hit me. "I think he means he's going to die."

"I bet you're right," Chookie said.

"Mr. Blackbird?" I called out.

No answer.

I called out again. Louder this time. "Mr. Blackbird, are you here?"

Silence.

"Maybe he's sleeping," Fish said.

"Let's check his coffin," I said.

We went into the living room. Mr. Blackbird's coffin was in its usual spot on the floor. The casket was closed, and I lifted the lid, and there he was. It looked like Mr. Blackbird was sleeping. I put a hand on his shoulder and shook him gently. When I placed my hand on his forehead, he was colder than an ice cube.

"He's dead," I said.

"This is creepy. Let's get out of here," Fish said, turning and bolting for the door, Chookie and I right behind him.

Once outside, I said, "Mr. Blackbird was a good man, and I'll miss him. We'd better tell Constable Tindell, and he'll know what to do."

With tears in our eyes, we ran straight to Constable Tindell's house. He didn't believe me when I told him the story of Mr. Blackbird's death. I pulled the letter from my pocket and handed it to him. After reading the note, he said, "I believe you now, David. I'll take care of it. You boys had better get on home."

As we left Constable Tindell's house, in all the confusion and panic, we had forgotten our pillowcases filled with treats at Mr. Blackbird's home.

"Let's go back and get them," I said.

"No way am I goin' back there," Fish said with a shudder.

"Me neither," Chookie agreed.

"Don't be chickens," I said. "I'll go in and get them. You two babies can wait outside."

"Okay," Fish said. "I don't wanna lose all those goodies."

"All right," Chookie said. "I'll go back as long as I don't have to go inside."

That night, it took a long time before I could fall asleep. When I finally dozed off, I had a dream of Mr. Blackbird. Like Mrs. Crookshank, I saw his spirit leaving his body and floating into the sky on his way home to a planet in a galaxy light-years away. I recalled my dream and smiled when I awoke, knowing Mr. Blackbird was returning home.

Alien?

B he first month of school flew by, and before I knew it, it was the last day of October. I awoke and looked out my bedroom window. I was surprised to see a light dusting of snow on the ground. It looked more like Christmas than Halloween. I thought the school day would never end. When I got home, I ate an early supper, changed into my costume, and rushed to Wally's

house. Chookie was already there. We were on another adventure, dressed as the Three Musketeers.

After knocking on doors for two hours, our pillowcases were bulging with candy, chocolate bars, and apples. Our last stop was the house on River Road. Mr. Blackbird had invited us to stop by, saying he had some "special treats" for us. All the other kids in town feared Mr. Blackbird and avoided his house like the plague. A sign on his front door read: *Welcome, boys! Please come in. Your Halloween treats are on the kitchen table.*

As we entered the front hallway, Fish said, "What kind of treats do you think Mr. Blackbird left for us?"

"I don't have a clue," Chookie said.

"There's only one way to find out," I said. "Let's go to the kitchen."

We found a handwritten note on the kitchen table and three envelopes with our names. I picked up the letter and began to read it out loud.

Dear Boys:

I want to thank you for all the help you've given me. You have been good friends in the brief time that I have known you. As a token of appreciation, I have left you each a little parting gift. It is time for me to leave earth and return to my home. Goodbye.

Sincerely,

Bonaparte Blackbird

We were shocked to find ten one-hundred-dollar bills in each envelope.

"Wow," Chookie said, his eyes wide with glee. "I can buy a lot of fishing gear with all this money, and maybe even a baseball glove and a pair of skates."

"Mr. Blackbird must be a rich man," Fish said, stuffing the money into his pocket.

"I agree. I wonder where Mr. Blackbird has gone?" I said.

"Maybe he went back to Muddy Water," Fish said.

"I don't think so," I said. "The note says Mr. Blackbird's leaving earth." Suddenly it hit me. "I think he means he's going to die."

"I bet you're right," Chookie said.

"Mr. Blackbird?" I called out.

No answer.

I called out again. Louder this time. "Mr. Blackbird, are you here?"

Silence.

"Maybe he's sleeping," Fish said.

"Let's check his coffin," I said.

We went into the living room. Mr. Blackbird's coffin was in its usual spot on the floor. The casket was closed, and I lifted the lid, and there he was. It looked like Mr. Blackbird was sleeping. I put a hand on his shoulder and shook him gently. When I placed my hand on his forehead, he was colder than an ice cube.

"He's dead," I said.

"This is creepy. Let's get out of here," Fish said, turning and bolting for the door, Chookie and I right behind him.

Once outside, I said, "Mr. Blackbird was a good man, and I'll miss him. We'd better tell Constable Tindell, and he'll know what to do."

With tears in our eyes, we ran straight to Constable Tindell's house. He didn't believe me when I told him the story of Mr. Blackbird's death. I pulled the letter from my pocket and handed it to him. After reading the note, he said, "I believe you now, David. I'll take care of it. You boys had better get on home."

As we left Constable Tindell's house, in all the confusion and panic, we had forgotten our pillowcases filled with treats at Mr. Blackbird's home.

"Let's go back and get them," I said.

"No way am I goin' back there," Fish said with a shudder.

"Me neither," Chookie agreed.

"Don't be chickens," I said. "I'll go in and get them. You two babies can wait outside."

"Okay," Fish said. "I don't wanna lose all those goodies."

"All right," Chookie said. "I'll go back as long as I don't have to go inside."

That night, it took a long time before I could fall asleep. When I finally dozed off, I had a dream of Mr. Blackbird. Like Mrs. Crookshank, I saw his spirit leaving his body and floating into the sky on his way home to a planet in a galaxy light-years away. I recalled my dream and smiled when I awoke, knowing Mr. Blackbird was returning home.

www.ingramcontent.com/pod-product-compliance
Lightning Source LLC
Chambersburg PA
CBHW080904120626
46555CB00008B/2956